Girl From
Hard Times Hill

This edition published 2014 by
A & C Black, an imprint of Bloomsbury Publishing Plc
50 Bedford Square, London, WC1B 3DP
www.bloomsbury.com

This edition copyright © 2014 A & C Black
Text © Emma Barnes 2014

The right of Emma Barnes to be identified as the author
of this work has been asserted by her in accordance with
the Copyrights, Designs and Patents Act 1988.

ISBN 978-1-4729-0443-0

A CIP catalogue for this book is available from the British Library.

Printed and bound by CPI Group (UK) Ltd, Croydon CR0 4YY

1 3 5 7 9 10 8 6 4 2

MIX
Paper from
responsible sources
FSC® C020471

The Girl From Hard Times Hill

EMMA BARNES

A & C BLACK
AN IMPRINT OF BLOOMSBURY
LONDON NEW DELHI NEW YORK SYDNEY

To Mum and Gill, with love

Contents

Chapter One

News

When Mum first told us, I couldn't believe it. I just sat there, with my mouth hanging open. Everyone else was making lots of noise. Nana and Grandpa were saying, 'That's wonderful,' and 'You've waited so long,' while the Littlies, Shirley and Barbara, were shrieking their heads off just to join in. (Shirley is five and Barbara is one: they both make a lot of noise even when they're not excited.)

Mum sat at the table with Dad's letter in her hand.

'I didn't want to tell you before,' she said. 'But now it's all settled! Not long, and he'll be back for good.'

My dad is in Germany at the moment. He's an aircraft engineer in the Air Force, and he's part of the Occupying Forces. It's their job to help get things straight, now that the War is ended, and help clear up the mess that Hitler left.

Mum and Shirley have moved around with Dad quite a bit – they even spent time in Germany. But I've always stayed in Wales, with Nana and Grandpa. This last year Mum has lived here too, so that Nana and Grandpa can help with the Littlies.

Now Dad's leaving the Air Force and coming home for good.

I caught Nana's eye across the room. She said, 'It's *wonderful* news, isn't it, Megan?'

'Oh, it is,' I agreed. 'Definitely.'

I was pleased. Really I was. I was relieved, too. You see, at first, when Mum said that she had something to tell us – big news from Dad – I had a horrible feeling that we might all be going out to Germany to live. Of course, I wouldn't have gone. I'd have insisted on staying. And in fact I'd never even have thought we might go, except that two days ago, my best friend, Pam, had said, 'You'll never leave me, will you, Megan?'

'Of course not,' I'd said, surprised.

'But what if your dad wants you all to go out to Germany?'

I'd laughed. 'That won't happen. I never went with them before, and I won't this time either.' I pointed at our street sign (we were walking home from school at the time). 'I'm Megan of Hardy Hill! And here I stay!'

Although it hadn't worried me at the time (Pam is a great one for dreaming up catastrophes that never happen), when Mum had said she'd something to tell us, something amazing – that she'd had a letter from Dad that morning – *well*. Suddenly I'd been scared that Pam knew something I didn't.

But it turned out everything was fine after all.

'Hooray!' Shirley yelled, jigging up and down. 'Dad's coming home! He's coming home!'

She went dancing round the kitchen. Mum got up and I was going to grab her but Shirley got to her first, so Grandpa took a turn with me, and then even Nana got up and waltzed round the room, while Grandpa did a jig with Barbara gurgling on his shoulder. It was washing day, and there were folded towels and sheets hanging on the drying line above our heads, and at one point Barbara grabbed a sheet and pulled it down. But everyone just laughed.

'I'm *so* pleased we're staying here!' I whispered to Nana. 'I'm never going anywhere else!'

'But, Megan – ' Nana began.

'What?'

'Oh, nothing. Just time for a cup of tea!'

It's always time for a cup of tea in our house: when something good happens, when something bad happens, or even just because, as Nana says, 'it's time for a nice sit down'. Grandpa always says that however bad rationing was during the War (and it's been worse since), Hitler would never have his way while the British could have their cuppa.

Nana took down the cake tin off the shelf. It's got a picture of Princess Elizabeth and her husband on the top, dressed in their wedding clothes. It said in the newsreel at the pictures that her dress had a train of silk thirteen feet long. My Uncle Harry says she shouldn't have had all those extra coupons to buy that dress, when everyone else is going short. He's a Communist, and doesn't believe in the Royal Family.

Nana doesn't agree. She says somebody's got to have nice things. It's like going to the pictures and watching the actresses in their glamorous outfits – it cheers everybody up.

Seeing that cake tin definitely cheered *me* up.

'Lemon cake!'

'I think the occasion calls for it,' said Nana. 'And blow the sugar ration!'

I wolfed down my tea and cake. I wanted to tell Pam my news. But then Shirley said something that stopped me short.

'Where's Dad going to sleep when he gets back?'

'He'll sleep with me, of course,' said Mum.

'But then where will *I* sleep?'

At the moment, Shirley sleeps in Mum's bed. Barbara sleeps in a cot squeezed in between the bed and the wardrobe.

'You'll be sleeping with Megan,' said Mum, as if it were the most natural thing in the world.

I spluttered on my last mouthful of tea. 'What!' I gasped, when I'd recovered. 'I'm not sharing with her!'

'Of course you are. There's plenty of room for both of you.'

'But that's not fair! It's *my* room!'

'Don't be silly,' said Mum. 'It will be great fun for you, sharing with your sister. You can cuddle up together at night. I loved sharing with my sister when I was young.'

Sometimes I think Mum doesn't understand me at all.

I looked at Nana. Nana *does* understand me, but this time she just shook her head quietly, and I knew that it was pointless to protest.

The trouble is, this isn't a big house, and there's always a lot of people in it. But I hated the idea of giving up my room. It's tiny, but I love it. I keep my comics in an old shoe-box, and my roller skates in pride of place on my chest of drawers. There's a model airplane that Dad once sent me hanging from the ceiling, my Royal Wedding mug, and the books I got last Christmas – my *School Friend* annual, *The Enchanted Wood* and *Five On A Treasure Island*. Even better, my room's got a little window looking over the back lane, and I can shout down to my friends, or watch the sunset over the rooftops or the swallows flitting back and forth.

Best of all, I can always escape from Shirley and Barbara.

The only hope was that Shirley would refuse to leave Mum.

No chance.

'I'd *love* to share with you, Megan,' Shirley said. 'We can play dollies *all the time*.'

It's funny how your mood can drop. My feet dragged as I carried plates and cups over to the sink. I don't really like changes. Now Dad was coming home *and* I was losing my room.

I was realizing something else, too. I've only ever seen Dad on leave. And for his last leave, Mum had gone out to visit *him*. In a way, I don't know Dad that well.

Nana washed and I dried.

'Nana,' I said after a while.

'Yes, love?'

'I've grown a lot since Dad was here, haven't I?'

'Yes, you certainly have.'

'What if – what if he doesn't really remember me? What if I don't really remember *him*?'

'What if, what if,' said Nana briskly. 'I never heard such nonsense. How did you feel last time, before he came?'

'I don't remember.'

'I'll tell you,' said Nana. 'You felt exactly the same.'

'Did I?'

'Yes. And then when he arrived, everything was fine.'

Nana can always make me feel better.

'Can I go and see Pam now?'

'Of course. But make sure you're back in good time – we're going to have sausages and fried bread for supper.'

It's usually just bread-and-jam on washing day.

'Don't worry,' I yelled. 'I'll be there!'

Chapter Two

Pam

I ran up the back lane to Pam's house, past yards which, like ours, were full of lines of fluttering washing. When I reached her gate, I called out 'Pammy-oh!' with my hands cupped round my mouth.

We all do that – the children who live on Hardy Hill. Whenever anybody wants a friend to come out and play, they call, 'Megan-oh!' or 'Tommy-oh!' or 'Susan-oh!' (the name changes, but you see what I mean) from the back lane. Then, whoever it is comes running out to find them.

We don't go into each others' houses much. Houses are full of grown-ups who don't want extra children under foot. So the funny thing is, although I see Pam every day, when I go into her house it's like visiting for the first time.

This time, Pam came to find me almost before I'd finished calling.

'At *last*,' she said. 'Mum made me help that awful Maureen with her spellings, or I'd have been round for you.'

One of the things Pam and I have in common is annoying siblings. We both dream of being only children. I suppose I *was* an only child, in a way, until Shirley and Barbara came back from Germany, and I often wish I still was. That's a secret, though – from everyone except Pam.

'So do we have time to go up the Hill?' Pam waved her roller skates at me. She was holding them by the straps.

'I reckon so!' I produced mine from behind my back.

'Come on, then!'

As we ran, we saw Davy Levenson sitting on his back step with a big book open on his lap. He peered at us but he didn't say anything. He never does say much, even though he speaks perfect English – he was born here, though his parents, who came from

Germany before the War, still sound German when they speak.

Pam paused a moment. 'Why don't you come roller-skating, Davy?'

Davy shook his head.

'Aw, come on! It's more fun than reading!'

Davy just shrugged so we ran on.

'That Davy – you'd think he'd like a change sometimes,' Pam grumbled. 'And my mum says reading isn't good for you.'

Pam's not a great one for reading herself. I *do* like reading, but I like to play out too. Reading is for evenings – curled up on my bed, all alone, with my little reading lamp on. Or at least, it was.

'It takes all sorts,' I said. This is something Nana often says.

'That's true. He is *strange*, though. Maybe it's because he's German.'

'He's not German.'

'You know what I mean. Or because he's Jewish.'

'I don't know,' I said. 'I don't know anyone else who's Jewish besides the Levensons.'

'My uncle lives in Cardiff and there's lots of Jewish people there. Do you know, he says some people don't like them?'

'I like the Levensons,' I said.

I did too. Davy was quiet – but that was better than some of the boys in our class, who made too much noise altogether. Mrs Levenson was always friendly to me. She asked me in sometimes on a Saturday, to light the gas on her stove. Apparently it's against her religion to light your own gas on a Saturday. She always asked if I was enjoying school, and sometimes gave me an apple.

I felt sorry for Mr Levenson. He was even quieter than Davy, with a haunted look about him. Sometimes he didn't even notice that I was there. Nana said a lot of his family had been killed by Hitler during the War.

'I like them too,' said Pam. 'And of course Davy's awfully clever,' she added, as if being clever was bound to make you a bit strange. 'I reckon he's even cleverer than my cousin's friend who went to grammar school.'

We had reached the railway bridge, and there was nobody around. I tugged Pam's sleeve. 'I've got something important to tell you.'

'What is it?' Pam turned and gazed at me anxiously. 'Is it something awful?'

'You always think it must be something awful!'

But when I told her the news about Dad, she gave a huge grin. 'Fabby-fantastic-scrumptious-delicious!' (That's what we say when we're really pleased about something.) We did the little clapping game ('ip dip a la ba da dutch cheese santa ma, santa ma alabada, sham!') that we do when we're happy, and then Pam said, 'Thank goodness! I was afraid you were going off to Germany and I'd never see you again.'

'Well, there's no danger of that.'

'Good, because I want us to be best friends forever.'

'Me too!'

We linked arms and sang our favourite song. It's one I learnt from Nana – she often sings it when she's doing housework. It's silly, but we like it.

'*Joshua, Joshua,*
Nicer than lemon squash you are.
Yes, by gosh you are,
Joshu-oshu-a!'

As we finished, a train came roaring up and we waited on the bridge until it was underneath and the steam came swooshing up through the gaps in the walkway, and then we screamed with laughter and ran on, arm in arm.

* * *

The Hill is a great place for roller-skating. It's a very smooth, steep road, and most importantly it only goes to the old Baptist Chapel so there are rarely any cars. Everyone who has roller skates likes to go there and do races. At the bottom there's a steep turn, and you have to be pretty skilful not to overshoot and land up in the blackberry bushes on the corner.

I love skating. I get asthma, which means I'm no good at most sports because I get out of breath, but that doesn't seem to matter on roller skates. Sometimes I go so fast I can feel the wind in my hair and I wonder if there are sparks flying from the wheels of my skates.

That evening I *almost* beat Pam's brother Tom, who is the roller-skate champion of our neighbourhood. Almost, but not quite. I *definitely* beat Pam, though she said a stone caught in her wheel. Pam is my very best friend, but she's not perfect – it's amazing how a stone sticks in her wheel every time she doesn't win!

Something really *did* catch in my wheel though, on my final race. I felt something jam, and then I heard a snap and my left foot was going all wrong. 'Look out!' I yelled to Peter Reece, who was racing me, and I veered across the road and landed with a thump on the grass next to the blackberries.

'Megan's hurt!' yelled Pam dramatically, and came rushing over to see if I'd broken anything.

'I'm alright,' I said gloomily. 'But look at my skate!'

A wheel had come off, and worse still, the metal holding it in place had snapped right through. We all tried but none of us could fix it.

'I'll get Grandpa to take a look at it,' I said, as we all set off for home.

Chapter Three

School

It was one of those afternoons when you'd rather be doing anything but sitting in school. It was cold for one thing, but Miss Bulmer had decided it wasn't cold enough to light the classroom fire. In front of me was a piece of lined paper with *Essay Topic: My Walk In the Countryside*, written across the top. What a stupid topic! We never went for walks in the countryside in our house. But that wasn't what was bothering me.

The fact is, the more time passed, and the more excited everyone became about seeing Dad, the less sure I felt. Nana had reassured me at the time. But now... It was *ages* since I'd seen him. Sometimes

I could hardly picture what he looked like. He was always joking, I remembered that. At least, everyone was always telling me that he was a great joker. But did I really remember? Or did I just think I did?

Shirley looked like Mum, everyone said so, and of course she had lived out in Germany, so Dad knew her really well. And everyone loved Barbara, with her dimples and ringlets (not that I could understand *why*, when she so often smelled of nappies and sick). But me… I was the ugly duckling of the family. And whenever I peered into the mirror, and saw my sandy hair scraped into two plaits, my freckled nose, and slightly crooked teeth, I didn't have the feeling that I was going to turn into a swan any time soon.

'Time to finish up, now,' said Miss Bulmer.

I jumped and quickly glanced at the clock. Twenty past three! How did that happen? And my paper was still as blank as when I started.

Ann Evans gathered all the essays and took them to the front. Then all the girls took out their knitting for ten minutes, and the boys drew, while Miss Bulmer read to us. It was a really dull book – nothing like as exciting as *Five on a Treasure Island*, or the other Famous Five books, which I had been getting out of the library. Also, I hate knitting squares, even if it is for refugees, and I don't see why the boys are allowed to draw instead.

But worse was to come. As the school bell began to clang, Miss Bulmer said in a stony voice, 'Megan Hunt and David Levenson, a word, please.'

My stomach lurched. When Miss Bulmer holds people back, it usually means trouble.

Pam wiggled her eyebrows at she filed past. I gave a tiny shrug. Trevor Pritchard murmured, 'Davy and Megan, up a tree, K-I-S-S-I-N-G – ' and then he saw Miss Bulmer's eye on him, and he shut up, sharpish.

I trudged up to Miss Bulmer's desk and stood next to Davy, waiting. The essay papers were piled on her desk. I could see the wooden ruler that she uses for rapping knuckles. She's never rapped my knuckles, but there's always a first time.

It seemed to take forever for everyone to leave. Then Miss Bulmer took her steel-rimmed spectacles off and polished them.

Miss Bulmer is quite old. She should have retired from teaching, people say, but because of the War, and all the evacuees, she stayed on. Now the War is over, but Miss Bulmer is still here. Some people say it's because she's discovered she enjoys torturing children too much to give it up.

Miss Bulmer picked up my essay – or rather, my blank piece of paper.

'Country walks don't appeal to you, evidently, Megan?'

'I'm sorry,' I whispered. I was sure I was going to get the ruler now.

'You will have to do a lot better than this – ' she was making such a sour face, just as if she were sucking a lemon, that I almost missed what she said next – 'if you are to have a chance of winning a place at grammar school.'

I was so surprised that I didn't know what to say.

'Well?' Miss Bulmer snapped.

'But – I'm not going to the Grammar,' I gasped.

'Is that so? And I had thought it was the examiners who would decide that, once you had taken the Eleven Plus exam.'

'I meant, I'm not clever enough.'

Miss Bulmer sniffed. 'I am a better judge of that!' She made it sound like an insult. 'Of course you will have to apply yourself. But there is time.'

Then Miss Bulmer turned her attention to Davy. '*You*, David, do work hard, but you sometimes get nervous during tests, I've noticed. So you need to practice too.'

She told us about some extra work she wanted us to do. We both nodded.

'Good,' said Miss Bulmer. She looked at us hard. 'I hope you both understand what an opportunity this is. If you do go to grammar school, it could change the course of your lives.'

We nodded obediently. But as we left the classroom, I realised I had no idea what she was talking about. Grammar school! I knew where the Girls' Grammar was – I'd walked past it from time to time with Nana, when we went shopping in town. I'd seen the girls coming out the gates, in their ugly pleated skirts and silly straw hats. Big girls, with piles of books under their arms. I didn't see what was so great about that.

The only other thing I definitely knew about grammar school pupils was that they learnt Latin. I had asked Grandpa about Latin once (there were Latin words written over the door of the library) and who spoke it, and he had said, 'A lot of dead Romans'. That didn't sound very useful to me.

'Well!' I said to Davy, as we walked across the playground. 'That was a surprise!'

Davy just smiled.

'Wouldn't you rather just go to the Secondary, like most people?'

Davy shook his head. I was going to ask him more, but as we walked out of the gates, Pam jumped out from behind a tree.

'Surprise!'

'Eek!' I squeaked.

'You've been *ages*! How mean of old Bully-Bulmer to keep you back! After all, you usually write loads and loads.'

I opened my mouth to explain, then shut it again. For there was one thing I knew for sure about grammar school – whether or not I was bright enough to get in, Pam would definitely never go. She's usually near the very bottom of the class.

Pam was looking at Davy. 'What did she keep *you* back for, Mr Clever Clogs?' Pam was smiling, though. It's not Davy's fault he's clever.

'It was about trying for the Grammar School,' replied Davy in a soft voice.

'Oh, you'll be sure to get in,' Pam said. 'Rather you than me!'

'Why's that?' I asked quickly.

'It's awful. I know all about it. My cousin's friend goes there.' As we walked up the street, past children playing skipping games, hopscotch or bouncing balls against the wall, Pam ticked off her points on her fingers. 'One: too much homework. Hours and hours of it, I've heard. Two: too many posh boys – or girls. They all speak with silly voices like this: "*Taime to have your tae, my dear!*" Three: it's so far to go – you'd have to get the bus each day. And worst of all, I'd miss all my friends. Thank goodness,' Pam finished cheerfully, '*I'm* not clever enough to go!'

I *was* going to tell Pam the truth. Honest I was. She's my best friend and best friends don't have secrets. But I hesitated, searching for the right words, and unfortunately Davy chose this moment, of all moments, to change his clam-like ways.

'Miss Bulmer thinks Megan could go to the Grammar.'

Pam turned to look at me, her mouth round with astonishment.

'I was as surprised as anything – ' I began, but Pam interrupted.

'You *pig*, Megan! You mean pig! You weren't even going to tell me! And then off you go to the lah-di-dah Grammar School! I'll never forgive you! Never! I wish you *had* gone to Germany!'

She turned and took off, almost trampling two little kids who were crouched in the gutter with their marbles. Pigtails bouncing, she went flying up the hill.

Davy said anxiously, 'I'm sorry, Megan.'

'You just keep your nose *out* of my business in future!' I snapped. Then I ran after Pam.

Chapter Four

Surprise!

I was quite despondent as I trudged up Hardy Hill later that afternoon.

I'd caught up with Pam, but she wouldn't listen. She just kept turning her back on me. Then she burst into tears, and when I tried to put an arm round her, she shoved me away. Finally she marched off, saying she was going to join the other kids roller-skating. She knows perfectly well that my roller skates are still broken.

So that was that!

All the way home, I kept thinking how unfair life was. It's not as if I *wanted* to go to the mouldy old

Grammar. And then I had a brain-wave. Who said I had to go? There's an exam that you do first, called the Eleven Plus. Miss Bulmer had said Davy and me would both need to work really hard to pass it. Well, what if I didn't do well enough? If I didn't try hard in the exam, then nobody, not even Miss Bulmer, could do anything about it.

I suddenly felt a lot more cheerful.

I was so deep in these thoughts that it took me a few moments to notice that the front door of our house was standing wide open – which it never does. And when I poked my head inside and called, 'I'm home!' nobody answered. But I could hear an absolute babble of voices from the back of the house.

My heart gave a big thump. Grandpa and Nana aren't as young as they were. A heart attack – an accident...

I started down the hall.

But when I arrived in the kitchen, it was to find Nana laughing; Grandpa smiling too, where he stood leaning against the mantelpiece; and Shirley chattering nineteen to the dozen. Meanwhile Barbara, like Mum, was clinging to the tall blond man who was standing in the middle of the room, dressed in the blue-grey Royal Air Force uniform.

My dad.

For what felt like a long time (though it could only have been a minute) nobody noticed me. I just stood in the doorway, fidgeting, and watching Mum rocking back and forth on my dad's chest, her face wreathed in smiles, and Barbara crowing cheerfully as she held on to my dad's little finger.

It was Nana that spotted me.

'Here she is! Here's our Megan!'

'Hello,' I said. For some reason, I suddenly felt shy. I just stood there, scuffing my feet on the lino.

Dad turned at once to look at me. I'd recognized him all right – but it seemed like it took him a moment to recognize *me*. I felt suddenly all awkward and gawky, very aware of how tall I've got in the last year, and how none of my clothes fit right. Nana had said they'd have to 'do' until we could save our pennies to get new ones.

'Megan!' He held his arms out. I walked slowly across the floor.

Dad passed Barbara to Mum, then made to swing me up, but stopped. 'You *have* grown,' he said. He sounded surprised. Then he gave me a hug instead. He tweaked one of my plaits, in a way that I hate (Shirley is *always* doing it) and peered down into my face. 'I left a little girl – and find this young lady!'

I muttered something.

'Look, Megan!' Shirley crowed. 'My present!'

It was a teddy bear – a gorgeous one, with soft velvet paws and an embroidered smile. I'd have liked it, I admit, even though I'm eleven.

'And Barb's got a new coat,' said Shirley. 'And Mummy's got some sweets she likes, and Nana has hankies and – '

I felt really hurt that they had all opened their presents without waiting for me.

Dad coughed. 'I've something for you, Megan, but I wonder…well anyway, here it is.'

I took the package and pulled off the paper. A doll. A baby doll, with yellow curls, blue eyes and a white dress. Beautiful, but…it's been *ages* since I played with dolls.

'Lovely,' Nana said. 'What do you say, Megan?'

'Thank you,' I whispered.

Dad said, 'When I bought that, I hadn't realized how grown-up you were now. I think you're maybe a bit old for it?'

'Maybe just a little…' I caught sight of Mum frowning at me.

'She's wonderful!' Shirley touched my doll's cheek tenderly.

'Shirley will enjoy playing with it, anyhow,' said Mum rather crossly.

It didn't seem very fair that Shirley should get a doll *and* a teddy. But I didn't say anything. I could see Mum thought I was ungrateful, but it wasn't my fault that Dad had forgotten how old I was.

'And here's something I brought for all of us. Try some of this!' Dad was rummaging in his knapsack. Finally he produced what he was looking for. We all stared at it.

'What's that?' Shirley asked.

'It's a banana, stupid,' I said. I knew that much. I'd occasionally seen other children eating them but I'd never tried one myself.

'Oh. D'you mean you eat it?'

''Course you do – if you're a monkey.'

Dad laughed. 'And even if you're a little girl. Come on, my three little monkeys. Want to try a piece?'

I didn't like being called a monkey. (The Littlies *are* monkeys, I have to admit.) And although I know what a banana looks like, I wasn't about to taste one, either.

'No, thanks.'

Dad just laughed. 'Go on, Megan.'

I took a little piece. It was all I could do not to spit it out.

'Yuk! I don't like it.'

Shirley didn't like it either. And as for Barbara – Barbara *did* spit her piece out, all over Dad's shoulder.

'You ungrateful children!' Mum laughed and ate a piece herself, but she looked annoyed. Nana ate some too. As for Grandpa – there wasn't any left by that time. But he said he didn't mind.

'A nice, crunchy apple is fine with me.'

Dad shook his head. 'To think of the care I've taken of that blessed banana, wrapping it up in my socks to make sure it didn't get squashed!'

'Oooh!' yelled Shirley. 'You wrapped it in your *socks*.'

'Adds flavour,' he said, grinning.

Nana said, 'Now, Bob – '

'Don't worry – they were clean socks!'

Shirley went on making faces, but Dad just leant over and ruffled her hair.

Grandpa went to get Dad's suitcase in, then, and to shut the front door. ('To think it's been open all the time', said Nana, 'letting in a draught.') Nana took the kettle off the range to brew a pot of tea. Mum kept fussing over Dad, and showing him how Barbara could walk now. Then Dad started doing tricks for Shirley, Barbara and me. He took a coin out from behind

Barbara's ear, and pretended to take his thumb off. He always used to do these tricks, and I remember loving them, just the way the Littlies do now. But somehow this time I couldn't get that excited: I *knew* it was a coin from his pocket, and I could see that he just had his thumb bent back when he pretended to take it off.

I did my best. I laughed, or tried to. But I'm not a very good actor. (I *never* get picked for school plays.)

'Look!' Dad wiggled his ears at me. I laughed politely. 'Want me to teach you?' he asked.

'Not really. It must be nice, though,' I added.

Dad looked a bit puzzled. I suppose Shirley would think it hilarious, somebody wiggling their ears, but you would have thought he would realize I was a bit old for that. Suddenly there was a lump in my throat. I swallowed and looked away.

I edged over to Mum. 'Do you think I could go and see Pam?' I whispered.

'Megan! When your dad's just got home!'

She turned away, and I didn't have a chance to explain. So I went to help Nana with the teacups. But my face was hot with shame and anger. It wasn't fair for Mum to be cross. The only reason I wanted to see Pam was to explain about the grammar school – so that she wouldn't still be thinking that I might pass the Eleven Plus and leave her to go to Secondary on her own. Anyway, as Dad obviously found the Littlies more fun than me, he wouldn't miss me.

Everything was changing, I thought gloomily, as I set out teacups and tried not to slop the milk. New schools, Dad coming home, arguments with friends. I wasn't sure I liked it.

Chapter Five

Making Plans

The next day I cornered Pam in the school playground.

'Listen,' I said, 'I'm not going to the stupid Grammar, so stop being angry!'

'That's what you *say*,' said Pam. 'But if Miss Bulmer says you are – '

'I'm going to fail the exam,' I told her. 'If I do as badly as I can, there'll be nothing she can do about it.'

'Oh.' Pam still looked doubtful. She scuffed her feet. 'Why didn't you come and say so yesterday, then? I was miserable, and you never came to find me!'

'I couldn't. They wouldn't let me go out.'

'Why not?'

'My dad came home from Germany.'

'What!' Pam gazed at me. 'Really?'

'Cross my heart. He's not going back, either. He's home for good.'

'Oh Megan – why didn't you say so before?' Pam flung her arms round me. 'That's really exciting! Are you terribly happy?'

'Yes, of course I am. Well, it does mean I have to share my room with Shirley now – and you can imagine what that's like. Awful.' I made a face. 'Last night she kept kicking me, and then she needed to go in the night, and she knocked the chamber pot and it slopped right over the rug. I had to fetch Nana to help clean it up. And everyone keeps fussing over Dad, and I think he's forgotten how old I am…but of course, it's marvellous,' I added quickly.

Pam began dancing around the playground.

'And now you'll never go to Germany, and we'll be best friends forever!'

'Does that mean you won't go roller-skating without me?'

'Oh.' Pam stopped with one leg in the air. 'Hmm. Well. I do *really* like roller-skating.'

'Yes, but what about me? I love roller-skating too! And Grandpa says my skates can't be mended, and it's ages till my birthday.'

Pam hesitated a moment. 'I'll tell you what. Whenever we go roller-skating, you can have shares in my skates. Half the time I'll use them, and half the time you can. What do you think?'

'Oh, Pam! That's really kind!'

There were tears in my eyes. I was so lucky to have such a good best friend.

I was a bit cooler with Davy when I saw him, though. He gave me a little smile when we were waiting to go into the classroom, but I ignored him.

As for Miss Bulmer – I felt her gimlet eye on me a few times, but I didn't take any notice. In fact I started whispering with Ann Evans, who sits next to me, and every time I caught Pam's eye across the aisle I started giggling, and in the spelling test I got three wrong, which is unusual for me. I thought I saw Miss Bulmer pursing her lips, but I didn't pay any attention. When I heard her stalking up the aisle though, I kept quiet. I didn't want a rap on the knuckles!

At dinner-time I went home as usual. I normally love dinner-time – Nana is a good cook, and Mum makes sure that the Littlies behave for once, and

Grandpa comes in from work and often Uncle Harry does too. Everyone always asks me what happened at school that morning. But today all the grown-ups were just talking, talking, talking with Dad the whole time.

'Do you think they really need all this help we're giving them,' Uncle Harry asked Dad, 'when we're still so short of everything here?' He meant the Germans. Dad looked serious and started talking about how bad things were in Germany, and then all the grown-ups started on about rationing, and when (if ever) things might get easier.

'Of course, they weren't any easier before the War – and I'd rather have rationing than the Great Depression,' said Nana tartly. I couldn't remember those times. I cleared my plate as quickly as I could, and escaped back to school.

* * *

Still, I began to get used to Dad being around. I didn't spend much time with him, as aunties and uncles and old friends kept dropping by to see him, so there were often grown-ups sitting round the kitchen table, chatting and smoking and drinking cups of tea, while music played on the radio.

Then again, quite often he and Mum would go out. I'd have thought Nana would have got fed up of them going gallivanting, Dad in his suit and Mum in her prettiest, least patched frock, and leaving the Littlies behind, but she didn't say so. Maybe she thought they deserved a treat.

One day I was walking back from the Hill alone. Pam had run on ahead, because she hadn't done her jobs at home, and I was so busy thinking about the last race that I didn't pay attention and walked straight into somebody coming out of the fish and chip shop on the corner.

'I'm sorry,' I said, and then I heard laughter and looked up.

'Don't you recognize your own father?'

I could feel myself blush. 'Sorry, I didn't see you.'

'No, you were away with the fairies. You alright, Megan? You look done in.'

'I *am* tired,' I said. 'But you see, Tom and me drew in the first round, and so we had to go again, and then Brian fell over after a cat ran out, so we had to do *that* round again and then – '

'Hold on!' Dad interrupted. 'First round of what?'

'Roller-skating. We have races over at the Hill.'

Dad scratched his head. 'Magic roller skates, are they?'

'What do you mean?'

'I mean, I can't see them. They must be invisible.'

'Well,' I retorted, 'I can't see any fish and chips, and you just came out of the chippy!'

Dad started to laugh and I found that I was laughing too. Then I explained that I always had to borrow Pam's roller skates and Dad explained that they were just putting a new batch of chips into the fryer, so that he'd had to wait.

'Does Nana know?' I asked doubtfully. 'We only ever have fish and chips on Fridays.'

'She was persuaded,' Dad told me. 'Anyway, today's a celebration.'

'A celebration of what?'

'You'll just have to wait and see,' said Dad with a wink. And he wouldn't tell me any more. 'Meanwhile, you can help me carry the grub. Come on. We can take a stroll while we're waiting.'

We set off down the hill.

Chapter Six

Talking to Dad

'So why don't you have your own roller skates?' Dad asked as we headed towards the path to the railway bridge.

'I did, but they broke.'

'Have you still got them?'

'Yes, but it's no good. Grandpa's already tried to mend them.'

'I could take a look.'

'Well – '

'After all, I *am* a mechanic. I've spent over ten years of my life mending aeroplanes.'

I looked at him hopefully.

'Do you think you could? It's awkward taking turns, and Pam's skates pinch my toes.'

Dad nodded. 'Hooray!' I yelled. Then I felt Dad was laughing at me again, so I said quickly, 'Did you go roller-skating when you were young?'

'Never knew there were such things. Don't remember anyone having them.'

We had reached the grassy embankment near the railway. It was quiet – most people were off home to their tea.

'So what did you do with *your* friends?' I asked.

'Well, we did have a go-cart once, that we made ourselves. But other than that...we didn't have much money to spare for toys, Megan. In fact, me and my friend John used to go round selling things.'

'Like what?'

'Buns, mainly. We'd get them from the bakers – specially any that were a bit squashed, or that he thought were going stale. Then we'd sell them in the streets, outside pubs or workplaces. We'd charge a little more than we paid, so that we could make some money on it.'

'That sounds fun.'

'Sometimes we'd take a bucket and collect horses' droppings off the streets. There were lots of horses then, pulling carts.'

'Ugh!' I turned my nose up, although Grandpa sometimes picked up horse droppings for his allotment.

'We'd get good money for horses' droppings. People used them for their vegetable patches.'

'And what did you do with the money?' I asked. I was almost ready to get into bun-selling myself. Maybe I could buy some new roller skates. (I was less keen on the horse droppings.)

'Gave it to my mother.'

'What! All of it?'

'Every penny. And that's all it was sometimes – a few pence. It wasn't much but it helped. You see, Mum had a struggle just to put food on the table.'

I thought about this. We were working-class, I knew that. Grandpa was a stonemason, and my uncles all did hard, manual work of one kind or another. There was never much money to spare. But, so far as I could remember, we'd always had enough to eat. Of course we all complained about sweets and meat being rationed, but then everybody else was in the same boat. In fact, Nana sometimes said it was only the well-off who felt really hard done by, because they had been used to buying what they wanted before the War.

'Were you really *poor*?'

'Cold, stony broke,' said Dad, grinning. 'Remember that story about the old lady making nail soup? That was us, but without the carrot and the onion and the ham-bone. My father was a sailor, and he'd often drunk his pay before my mum could get hold of it. But then, nobody had much. They were hard times, Megan, even before the Great Depression. And when that struck there really were no jobs to be had. Lines of unemployed people, and women and children, holding mugs outside soup kitchens.'

'Nana said there was a soup kitchen at the chapel at the top of our street,' I said, remembering. 'There would be a queues of people stretching all down the street. People used to call it Hard Times Hill.'

Dad nodded. 'It *was* hard. Until the War. Then, at least, people had work to do.'

'What was it like, being in the War?' I asked. I'd always been curious, but I'd never liked to ask.

'D'you know what, more than anything, it was *boring*.'

'Boring!' I was shocked. 'How could a war be boring?'

'Well, it was for me. I played more card games, and whittled more bits of wood, and read more dog-eared paperbacks, than I hope I ever will again in my life.'

I thought about the boys I knew playing tank battles on the waste-ground. Or Pam and me, pretending to fly Spitfires. Or the films I'd seen at the pictures – they made the War look exciting all right.

'I suppose that was because you were a mechanic.'

Dad shook his head. 'No. It was boring for lots of people. Even if you were a fighter pilot, say – and I knew lots of those – there was always a lot of sitting around, until things got interesting – sometimes a lot *too* interesting.' Dad looked grim. 'A lot of those boys never came back. But a lot of the War was just one long, boring, lonely wait: waiting for the next plane to fix, waiting for parts for the plane, waiting for fuel, waiting for letters from home, waiting for food parcels from home, waiting for the next leave, the next cigarette. Not that I'm complaining,' he added. 'Believe me, if you *have* to be swept up in a war – and I hope to God you never will, Megan – then a boring war is the one to have. A lot of people in Europe starved, or – like the Levensons – had to leave their country behind forever.'

'Nana always says we were lucky,' I ventured. 'We weren't bombed. Not like in the big cities.'

'We've been very lucky,' said Dad.

We stopped at the top of the railway bridge. Dad looked thoughtful.

'Of course,' he said, 'in another way, the Air Force was a wonderful thing for me. It trained me up as a mechanic, gave me a trade. Took me to new places. Even the quiet times – we used to read and talk politics, as well as play cards. We talked about how things could be after the War. Then, when we got a chance, we voted for Mr Attlee and the Labour Party – a new way of doing things.'

'Nana voted Conservative,' I said.

Dad pulled a face. 'She's a wonderful woman, your grandmother, but she's not always right.'

Actually, I thought Nana usually was right. But I knew that she was unusual in voting Tory. Most people we knew, including Grandpa and all my friends' parents, voted Labour.

'So what's the new government doing that's so wonderful?' I asked. 'Everything's still rationed. Everyone's always complaining.'

'A lot of good things. A better deal for workers. And there's a new National Health Service, for one thing.' He punched me lightly on the shoulder. 'But enough of this high-flown political talk. We'd better get back. Or they'll be wondering at home whether we've run off with the chips!'

Chapter Seven

Bombshell

I love fish and chips. I eat them steaming hot out of their newspaper package, with a sloshing of vinegar and a good shake of salt, and I don't mind if the newspaper ink comes off on my hands. I think we all felt the same that evening. Shirley was licking her fingers, and Nana never even troubled to tell her off, while Dad was teasing Barbara by pretending her chip was an aeroplane, and then flying it into her mouth.

'Thank God they never put fish and chips on the ration!' said Grandpa, folding up the empty newspaper carefully. Later Shirley and me would cut it up into squares (the outer layers anyway) and Nana would thread them onto a string and hang them up next to the toilet.

Dad brought out a paper bag. 'And here's a little something I bought earlier to finish up. After all, this is a special occasion, isn't it, Megan?'

The bag was full of cream buns.

'Fish and chips *and* buns,' said Nana disapprovingly, but everyone else was already falling on them, so Nana stopped disapproving and got her own bun, quick.

'Wot speshul cashun?' asked Shirley with her mouth full.

'You'll have to wait and find out.' I felt rather smug that I'd known there was a secret, and Shirley had not.

'Go on, tell us, lad!' said Grandpa to Dad. And everyone else went, 'Yes, go on!'

Dad looked round the table. We were all quiet, even Barbara – although that might have been because her mouth was stuffed with bun.

'Well, then,' said Dad. 'You all know Mum and I went up to Newcastle a few days ago. Well, I was going to see the manager of an aircraft factory. Just to see if there were any posts coming up for somebody like me, who knows about engines. He said he'd let me know. Anyhow, today I got a letter. I've got the job, and it's at a good salary, too.'

While everyone was exclaiming, I sat quietly. I hadn't realized that Dad was looking for *work*, when he went off with Mum. I'd thought they were just off on a jaunt.

But it made sense. Of course he would have to find a job, now that he had left the Air Force. It was a shame, though, that he couldn't work here in Llanelli. Especially as I was just beginning to get to know him.

Now Mum was talking. 'We went to look at some houses while we were up in Newcastle. We saw a couple we liked, and we can afford the rent. It's all settled. At the end of this month, we'll be off!'

So Mum and the Littlies were going too. Well, I'd miss them (sometimes). But at least I'd get my room back.

Mum was telling everyone about her favourite house. 'Small, but sunny, very light, and three good bedrooms. Shirley and Barbara will share and Megan, you can have your own little room. It's small but you won't mind that.'

'That's really nice of you,' I said, 'but I don't mind sharing. It's not really fair for me to have a whole room, when I'm hardly going to be there.'

They all stopped yakking then and stared at me.

That was when I got the fluttery feeling in my stomach. Something was not right.

Mum said impatiently, 'What d'you mean – *hardly going to be there*? It's your new home!'

It was as if somebody had tipped a bucket of water all over me. Really, it was. I felt ice-cold and my hands were shaking. Yet at the same time, something was burning in my chest. I thought I might throw up.

When I spoke I could hardly get out the words.

'But – *I'm* not going to Newcastle. I'm staying here.'

'Don't be daft, Megan,' said Dad gently. 'Of course you're coming.'

'No! You don't understand. I mean,' I gabbled, 'I'll come and *visit* you. 'Course I will. Nana and Grandpa and me'll come on the train. But I can't *leave*. It's just like when you all went out to Germany. It's *exactly* the same. This is my home. I'm Megan of Hardy Hill!'

'Germany was different, Megan,' said Dad.

'Of course it was,' Mum agreed. 'We all knew Dad would be coming home one day. And now he's back for good, and we're all going to live together, like a proper family. Of course you're coming too.'

I could feel the rage rising inside me, like a volcano before it erupts. I leapt to my feet.

'No!' I shouted. 'I won't! And if you loved me at all, you wouldn't ask me to! Nana and Grandpa are my family! I'll never live with you! I hate you!'

There were tears streaming down my face. I ran out of the kitchen and slammed the door.

Chapter Eight

Nana Speaks Up

I lay on my bed sobbing into the pillows. I had never felt so miserable. 'I won't go,' I said aloud. 'I won't! I won't!' My life was here, with Nana, Grandpa and Pam. I belonged on Hardy Hill through thick and thin – hard times and good. If they tried to make me go, I'd run away!

After a long while, I began to calm down. I found a clean handkerchief and blew my nose. It occurred to me that nobody had come upstairs to comfort me – not even Nana. Were they *really* angry? Nana and Grandpa never lost their temper. Not like Pam's father, who got into terrible rages sometimes, and hit his children. What about Dad? Might he be the same?

I sat on the bed, with my arms wrapped round my knees. I wondered if the grown-ups were still talking downstairs. I wondered what they were saying about me. Maybe I should go and listen?

I got up, very quietly, and went to open the door.

Shirley was standing there, just outside the doorway.

'How long have you been there?' I hissed.

Shirley ignored this. 'You've been crying.'

'I know!'

'Why don't you want to come with us, Megan?'

'Because – because I'll miss here too much.' It was the truth, and my voice wobbled at the thought.

At that moment, I heard a voice from downstairs. Nana. 'Come down now, Megan. We want to talk to you.'

I swallowed. Then I glared at Shirley. 'I'm *not* going to say sorry,' I told her. 'And I'm not going to Newcastle either!'

In the kitchen, they were all sitting round with solemn faces. They had been drinking more tea. Like I said, always tea in a crisis.

Mum was looking cross. Everyone else just looked serious and a bit sad.

'Megan,' said Dad, 'we've been having a long talk, and we've decided not to go to Newcastle.'

I gasped. This was the last thing I had expected.

Mum said, 'And you needn't think it's anything to do with the way you've behaved this evening!'

Dad said, 'Your nana has been explaining that there are reasons why it's important you stay here. And I don't think we should split up the family at the moment. So we're all staying.'

'Oh, thank you, Nana,' I gasped. I should have known she would understand. But she was looking very solemn and suddenly I felt uneasy, all over again.

Nana said, 'I had a conversation with Miss Bulmer recently, Megan.'

'Miss Bulmer?' I couldn't see what she had to do with it.

'Yes. She told me that you have a good chance of passing the Eleven Plus and going to grammar school. *If*, that is, you really knuckle down and work hard.'

'But – ' I was confused. 'What's that got to do with Newcastle?'

'This isn't a good time for you to make a move, with the Eleven Plus coming up. So your mum and dad have decided that the family should all stay together for the moment.'

'There will be other jobs,' said Dad. I couldn't tell if he was cross or not. Mum sniffed, though, when he said it, which made me feel she didn't agree.

'Oh,' I said. I almost added, *But I'm not going to pass the Eleven Plus and I'm definitely not going to the Grammar,* but I managed to stop myself in time.

'But Megan,' Nana said, 'you have to understand. Your parents do need their own home, and their own lives, and when they do make a move, you will have to go with them.'

I said nothing.

'And the other thing is, we all expect you to work hard for this exam. Miss Bulmer told me that she spoke to you about it a few weeks ago, but she's not convinced that you're taking it seriously.'

I blushed. I knew just how bad my work had been.

'So, you must *promise* us that you will do your very best in the exam.'

I hesitated.

'Look at me, Megan,' said Nana sternly. So I lifted my chin and looked straight into her dark brown eyes, and I promised.

As I went back upstairs to bed, I reflected that I would have to work hard at school now. I couldn't break a promise to Nana. I just couldn't. Besides she would know – she always did. You couldn't lie to Nana.

Still, maybe I wouldn't pass the exam however hard I tried. Most people didn't. And if by some fluke I did do well enough to go to Grammar – well, it would be worth it, to stay here. Pam would understand. After all, I would be able to see her a lot more than if we went to Newcastle.

As for the bit about living with Mum and Dad eventually, I wasn't going to worry too much about *that*. Maybe Dad would find a job right here. If he did, then even if we moved house, I'd be able to spend almost as much time at Nana's as I did now. Anyway, that was months and months away, if it happened at all.

* * *

After that, everything sort of got back to normal. Sort of – but not really. For one thing, Nana was firm that I had to come straight home from school and do my homework before I could go out to play. So if Pam and the rest were dawdling, or going round by the allotments or the railway bridge, then I couldn't go with them.

I got into the habit of walking back with Davy Levenson. We would talk about homework, and the books we were reading from the library. Davy had read a lot of my favourite books, and some others too: *Wind in the Willows* and *Swallows and Amazons*. He told me that he sometimes read them aloud to his father, which surprised me. Davy said that his father was always thinking about the terrible things that had happened in the War, and the whole family was always trying to find ways to cheer him up. It was one of the reasons that Davy didn't play out much.

I still liked to play out though, and I'd race through my homework so that I could meet Pam. It also meant I could avoid spending time with Mum and Dad. I was sure they blamed me for not being able to move to Newcastle. I reckoned that was why Dad had never mended my roller skates, either.

Then one Saturday morning, I went to the pictures. I was sitting next to Pam in the sixpenny seats, and the Western had just finished (the cowboys had won, as usual) and in the gap before the cartoon, Pam's brother Tom leaned over and said to me, 'Was it your dad I saw selling dog food down Victoria Street?'

I was so taken aback, it took me a moment to reply. Then I said, 'I don't think so. He's an aircraft mechanic.'

'Well, it looked like him,' said Tom. 'He was going door-to-door.'

I didn't say any more. *Tom and Jerry* came on, and I was too busy laughing with everyone else. But when I got home later, and almost tripped over some tins of dog food piled up inside the back door, I remembered.

I stared at the tins with a peculiar feeling in my stomach. I'd wanted Dad to find work locally. And there was nothing *wrong* with selling dog food. Of course there wasn't. But I'd always been very proud of the fact my dad fixed aeroplanes. Selling dog food was a bit of a come-down.

It was at that moment that I heard voices from beyond the scullery door.

'...don't see why we couldn't have gone to Newcastle.'

'Gwen, you know why, we agreed that Megan's education should come first.'

'I still don't see why she couldn't just take the Eleven Plus in Newcastle. Or join us later. Anyway, she might not even pass, and who knows if you'll ever get another chance?'

I felt tears stinging my eyes. So they *did* blame me. Dad had given up his new job; Mum had lost the chance of her own home. And it was my fault.

I turned towards the back door. But my foot caught on one of those wretched tins, which fell to the floor with a clang. Before I could escape into the yard, the door opened, and Dad peered through.

'That you, Megs? Was wondering if there was a specially big mouse clattering about in there. Come on in. In fact, if you've got a moment, why don't you show us what you've been set for your homework this week?'

Dad's eyes were very sharp, but if he'd noticed my tears he didn't say anything. I was glad to bend my head over my homework books.

To my surprise, it really helped, concentrating on mental arithmetic, and I stopped feeling like I was about to cry. Dad turned out to be very good at sums – and very patient too. When we closed the book, he said that we'd practice every day from now on.

Upstairs in my room, though, I felt awful. I was sure, on top of everything else, that he and Mum thought I'd been eavesdropping. And with Shirley sitting in the middle of my rug, playing 'school' with her dolls, I couldn't even have a quiet cry.

Chapter Nine

Disaster

The day before the Eleven Plus, Miss Bulmer said that we weren't to fret or feel nervous, just to come to school after a good breakfast next morning, and do our best. She also said that we shouldn't do any homework that evening, but something completely different. So when Pam came running up, and said there was going to be a big race against the Copperworks Terrace lot over at the Hill that afternoon, I didn't think twice.

'I can share your skates, can't I?'

''Course you can,' said Pam at once. (Sometimes she had been a little reluctant to share, but I guess with a big contest against the Copperworks Terrace lot she knew we needed every good skater we had.)

We linked arms and ran for the gates. And that was when I spotted Mum through the railings. She was wearing her Sunday best frock and hat, and she had Shirley by one hand.

'Oh, there you are,' she said, when I came up. 'I need you to mind your sister.'

'But I'm just off out with Pam!'

'Not today you're not. I'm going to meet Dad now off the Cardiff train, and I want you to take Shirley and look after her until your Nana gets back. She's taken Barbara to visit Aunt Ada. Grandpa's still at work.'

'Oh, Mum!' I wailed. 'Can't she go with you?'

'No. Dad and I are going to have a nice afternoon tea – we don't want a grizzling five-year-old with us today.'

'Neither do I,' I muttered.

Mum pursed her lips. For once she looked quite like Nana. 'That's enough cheek from you, young lady. You do little enough to help with your sisters. Now, if Shirley's hungry she can have some bread and butter, but no cake until your Nana gets back. And go out with her to the toilet if she needs to go – you know she's scared of the spiders.'

I glowered. But the next moment, I was holding Shirley's sticky hand, and Mum was walking briskly down the street.

'Why did Dad have to go to Cardiff?' I groaned. 'I'm going to miss the race now.'

Pam looked at Shirley thoughtfully. 'Can't we take her with us?'

I paused. I knew perfectly well Mum had meant for me to take Shirley home and look after her there. But she hadn't actually *said* I couldn't take Shirley to the Hill. Besides, *she* was off out with Dad – to a fancy tea shop, too – and they'd never even thought of taking me. So why should I worry?

'She'll never know,' Pam urged. 'Come on, Megan!'

So we both grabbed a bewildered Shirley by the hand, and started for the Hill. Pam shouted to Tom to fetch her skates from home when he got his own, and by the time we got to the Hill (Shirley was a bit of a slowcoach) Tom was already there, with a load of other kids from our neighbourhood.

'Now, you sit here, and don't move,' I told my sister, finding her a nice big stone to sit on.

Shirley gave me an angelic smile. 'I like watching races.'

'Don't go wandering off, alright?'

'Don't worry, I'll help keep an eye on her,' said Pam encouragingly.

It was wonderful skating that afternoon. We raced off against each other, and counted up our wins. I was doing great, though I couldn't help wishing that Pam's skates didn't pinch my toes. I knew I'd have done better in my own skates.

As for Shirley, she watched for a bit, then started collecting pebbles. That seemed a nice, harmless activity so I left her to it.

A bit later, I was sitting at the very bottom of the hill, completely absorbed in watching Tom race Brian Hughes from Copperworks Road. I knew that whichever of them won, *I'd* be racing next. And whoever won that race would be the overall winner. Pam was already out of the contest. She was sitting close to Shirley, and arguing with Mary Black about something: I could hear their raised voices. I held my breath and watched Tom come round the bend…

…And it was at that moment that a scruffy little terrier dog ran onto the road. Somebody said later that it was the dog that belonged to the caretaker at the Chapel. Anyway, he went bouncing out in front of Tom, tail wagging. This wouldn't have mattered so much – but Shirley ran out after him.

Tom was already veering to miss the dog: he went smack bang into Shirley instead. She went flying into the air. And when she landed her eyes were shut and she didn't open them.

Chapter Ten

Waiting

I sat with my feet squashed up on the chair in front of me, and my arms wrapped round my knees. All around was a hospital smell of chemicals and disinfectant. Sometimes a nurse or doctor would go past, and normally I would have been interested to watch what they were doing. But today I stared at the clock on the wall. Its hands seemed to move incredibly slowly.

But maybe that was better. At the moment, I didn't know if I wanted time to pass.

My eyes slid to the door a bit further along the corridor. It was shut. Sooner or later, somebody would come through. Then I would find out. Then I would know, one way or the other, whether I had maimed – or even killed – my sister.

I tried not to think about what had happened, but it kept forcing itself before my eyes. Brian and some of the others had run for help, while I knelt next to Shirley. I could hear Tom saying in a choked voice, 'It was my fault, if only I'd braked quicker – ' and Pam, sobbing, 'It was me, I was sitting right by her – I'm so sorry, Megan!' But I knew that neither of them was to blame. *I* was the one who was supposed to be looking after Shirley. It was my fault.

The door opened, and my heart gave a sudden, painful jolt, but it was only a nurse. She didn't even glance at me, just walked briskly up the corridor, her neat blue skirt swishing as she walked. I didn't dare stop her to ask how Shirley was doing.

I wished Nana was here. But she had gone back home to look after Barbara. I could have gone home too, but I didn't want to. I needed to be here, in the hospital, waiting.

Nana had brought me some knitting to take my mind off things, and a cheese sandwich wrapped in greaseproof paper. But I couldn't knit and I certainly couldn't eat.

The door opened. The doctor came out, looking very serious, with his spectacles perched on his nose. Dad followed. He looked dead tired. His good suit, the one he had been wearing on his trip to Cardiff, was all crumpled.

As they approached, I couldn't help it – I started to tremble. Dad squatted down next to me. 'Megan, they think she's going to be fine. She's sleeping now.'

'Oh,' I gasped. 'Oh.' And then I couldn't help it: I burst into floods of tears.

Dad put an arm round me. The doctor patted me on the shoulder. 'I'll send a nurse with a nice cup of tea,' he said. 'You mustn't worry too much about your little sister.' Then he moved on up the corridor.

'Can I see her?' I asked Dad.

'It was hard enough persuading the Matron to let Mum stay. She's a dragon, that Matron, I can tell you – a real Tartar! But maybe when Shirley wakes up you can pop in for a minute. Or would you rather I took you home?'

'I want to wait.'

Dad sat down next to me and then got up quickly, rubbing his behind. 'Ouch – what's that?'

'It's my knitting needles,' I said. We both laughed, rather shakily, as Dad tucked the knitting needles away amongst his and Mum's coats and bags. Then he dug around in his pocket and found a rather crumpled cotton handkerchief. I took it and mopped my eyes.

The nurse came over with cups of tea for both of us, very hot and sweet. I sipped mine, and thought about Nana saying, 'Whatever the crisis, you can't beat a nice, hot cuppa.' That almost made me burst into tears again.

After a while, I said in a smothered voice, 'It was all my fault.'

'Well, I don't know,' said Dad. 'It was partly that dog's fault.'

'No, it was mine. Mum never said I could take Shirley out.'

'That's true, Megan. But then again, Mum's been saying it's all *her* fault for letting you be in charge when you're only eleven.'

I shook my head. 'The worst thing,' I said with a gasp, 'is that sometimes I've wished Shirley *would* die. Well, not that she'd be *killed* exactly. But I've definitely wished she'd never been born.'

I waited for Dad to recoil in shock and horror. To my surprise, he laughed.

'I know just how you feel. *I* once pushed my little brother into a canal. I was really disappointed when my best friend fished him out again.'

I giggled. I couldn't help it. 'What had he done?'

'Oh, getting up my nose as usual, I expect. Believe me, Megan, everyone has those feelings.'

I felt a lot better. But then something else occurred to me. Something almost as bad.

'Dad, what about the doctors' bill?'

Whenever somebody was ill, and they had to call out the doctor, Nana and Grandpa always worried about paying the bill. And Shirley was actually staying in hospital – that must be horribly expensive. And maybe Mum and Dad couldn't pay. Dad had given up that good job in Newcastle…he couldn't earn much selling dog food…and it was all my fault again…

With these thoughts jittering round my head, I almost missed Dad's reply.

'Well, as it happens, Megan, you've chosen a good time.'

'What do you mean?'

'You must know there's a National Health Service now. We don't have to pay a penny.'

I twisted round to look at him. 'Really? We don't have to pay *anything*?'

'No. It's a wonderful thing. I remember what people used to suffer, all because they couldn't afford a doctor.' Dad put his arm around me. 'All the same,

Megan, I'd as soon we didn't make use of our new National Health Service *too* often, if it's all the same to you.'

I knew he was teasing. I managed a small smile, but then something else occurred to me.

'I bet Mum's mad with me, isn't she? And I know you didn't want to stay here. You're both angry with me, because you wanted to go to Newcastle. It was only Nana persuaded you to stay.'

'You're wrong, Megan.' Dad looked serious again. 'Shall I tell you something? When I was your age I was good at my schoolwork, especially figures. But there wasn't money for me to go to the Grammar, even though I passed the exam, not even enough to buy the uniform. I had to leave school and join the Air Force as soon as I could. Now you've got this chance at an education, and I'm going to make sure you take it.' He paused. 'It wasn't Nana persuaded us. It was me.'

'Oh,' I said. Then, to my surprise, I told him something I hadn't even told Nana. 'The truth is, Dad, I don't want to go. I mean – I am working hard, like I promised, but I don't want to be at a different school from Pam. We've been best friends since forever.'

'It is hard,' Dad agreed. 'Life is hard sometimes. And maybe it shouldn't be that way. But as you've got this chance, then you must take it, Meggy.'

'And – do you really not mind selling dog food?'

'Not for the moment. But I do need a more secure job.' He looked at me sideways. 'That's why I was in Cardiff today. I was meeting an old Air Force chum, but I was also finding out about opportunities there. Your mother and I were having tea to talk things over. We think that once you've taken your Eleven Plus, *if* you pass, you could transfer to a good school in Cardiff, and I'd be able to get a decent job. I know you'll miss Nana and Grandpa, and your friends too, but you'd still be able to see them sometimes. It's much closer than Newcastle.'

He was being really kind. Besides, after all that had happened, I couldn't refuse to go.

'All right,' I muttered.

'Mum and I know it's hard. But we want us all to be a family again.'

I nodded. Then I leaned my head against Dad's shoulder.

After that we just sat quietly. For a while I brooded about moving to Cardiff, but then, to distract myself, I started looking around the hospital. It was an interesting place. Through an open door, I could see a young man having his hand stitched. A nurse was pouring some kind of medicine into a bottle through a funnel. Two doctors walked past, deep in discussion of the operation they were due to perform in the morning.

'I wouldn't mind being a doctor,' I said, surprising myself. 'I'd like to do operations.' Then I blushed and waited for Dad to laugh at me.

'Well, if you go to the Grammar, anything's possible.'

'*Really?*'

I thought it was one of his jokes. But he said seriously, 'Yes, really, Megan.'

'But girls don't do things like that. Or anybody we know.'

'Things are going to be different now. Anyway, if you want to do it, then I'll be behind you all the way.'

I thought about this. If I could be a doctor one day… Well, maybe it would be worth putting up with the silly uniform and the homework, or even going to a different school from Pam. I sighed.

'Everything's changing.'

'I know,' Dad agreed. 'But some things stay the same. That reminds me…' He began rummaging among the coats and bags that he and Mum had left on the seat next to me. 'I told you I went to see a mate of mine in Cardiff. He's just come home from Germany too. I asked him to bring me something.'

He handed me a package. I pulled off the brown paper and opened the box.

'Roller skates!'

Dad grinned. 'Yours were past repair, I'm afraid. So I wrote and asked my mate to bring some back.'

I examined them. 'They look different.'

'That's because they're from Germany. We've beaten them in two World Wars, but they're still marvellous engineers. I reckon these will be a great little pair of skates.'

'Do you mean I can still go skating?'

'Well, you can't waste them, can you? But,' Dad added judiciously, 'it might be wise to keep them out from under your mother's nose. And your grandmother's. Maybe after the Eleven Plus – '

And that's when it struck me.

'It's the Eleven Plus tomorrow!'

'Right,' said Dad briskly, glancing at his watch. 'Let's get you home straight away!'

Chapter Eleven

Cardiff

Four months later, I sat on the top deck of a Cardiff bus, peering out of the window at the smoggy, unfamiliar Cardiff streets, feeling absolutely awful.

It seemed such a long time ago since I'd left Nana and Grandpa's. It wasn't, really – but it already felt like a different life.

It had been such a wonderful summer, after school had finished. Dad had found a job in Cardiff, and he and Mum and Barbara had moved into a flat there. Shirley and I were to join them in time for the new school term, once they had settled in and got everything straight. But in the meantime, it had been just like the old days. I was out with my friends every day from dawn to dusk, skating or climbing trees. We'd be hanging around Mrs Morgan's shop every Wednesday to be first to get a copy of *Crystal* or *School Friend* (Tom would be waiting for *Dandy* or *The Beano*) and going to the pictures every Saturday morning and sometimes midweek too. In the evenings, after Shirley had gone to bed, it was just me and Grandpa and Nana, listening to the radio or reading. Even though I knew it wouldn't last forever, I almost believed it would.

Only, as Nana says, 'all good things come to an end'.

The goodbyes had been the worst thing. Pam's was the noisiest. She sobbed all over me, and gave me her precious white rabbit's foot that she claimed brought her good luck. I'd given her my roller skates. It was a real wrench, but I wasn't sure I'd be able to use them in Cardiff. They were fantastic skates – Dad had been right about that. 'They're still yours!' Pam wailed. 'I'll just look after them!' Then we hugged and promised we would always be best friends.

Davy Levenson had come round and given me his copy of *Swallows and Amazons*. I'd been all tongue-tied at first, and just stood there, blushing. For it hadn't been a wonderful summer for the Levensons. It had been a terrible one. Not long after Davy had got the wonderful news that he had come top of the whole county in the Eleven Plus, Davy's father had killed himself. Nobody had known how to understand it. And while it was dreadful, of course, nobody had known Mr Levenson very well, for he never went down to the pub for a drink like most men, or stood chatting on the pavement. I knew Nana had taken flowers and cake to Mrs Levenson. But, like most people, I'd hardly seen Davy or his family since.

'Thank you,' I'd whispered, taking the book. And then I'd blurted out, 'I'm so sorry about your dad.'

Davy just nodded.

'How's your mum doing?'

'Better.' Davy was looking very white and thin, and there were shadows under his eyes.

'It's awful for you. Sometimes, these last months, I've felt *I* was living on Hard Times Hill. But I never was, really. It's you that's had the hard times.'

Davy said nothing for a while, and I was worried that I'd offended him. But then he said, 'It's been bad. But the truth is, Dad's never been happy since the War. He was always thinking about the people left behind.'

I nodded. I'd known for a while that the Levensons had relatives and friends in Germany, and that many of them had been killed in the concentration camps. But it had never seemed real until now.

'Mum's trying to decide whether we should stay in Wales, or whether we should make a new start. Some of her relatives from Germany live in Israel, now – you know, that people used to call Palestine.'

'I hope you stay,' I said, and Davy said he hoped so too. He liked Wales, he said, and he was looking forward to grammar school, and besides, he didn't want to have to speak a different language.

After he had gone, I realized that I was going to miss Davy far, far more than I would ever have expected.

Strangely enough, I was going to miss Miss Bulmer too. She had given me a lovely diary with a leather cover to write things in, and I had given her a homemade bookmark with a picture of an owl on it.

Of course, the very worst goodbye was to Nana and Grandpa.

The night before I left, Nana helped me pack. Then first Shirley then I had a bath in front of the fire: Grandpa bringing in the metal tub from the coal shed, and filling it up with kettles of hot water from the range, and Nana helping to scrub our backs and wash our hair, although I am really too old to need a helper at bath-time. Then, when Shirley was all tucked up in bed, and Grandpa was emptying the bath tub in the yard, I sat wrapped in a towel in front of the flames, while Nana brushed my hair.

'I can't do it!' I cried suddenly. Everything blurred as the tears rose up behind my eyes. 'I want to stay with you!'

'I know just how you feel,' said Nana gently.

'No you don't! You can't!'

'Don't you remember,' Nana said, 'that I once went to Cardiff myself?'

Of course I knew. Nana had often told me about how she had gone into service after she'd left school, and left her own family in the countryside and lived as a servant in Cardiff.

'That was different,' I said impatiently. 'You were *much* older!'

'I was twelve. Hardly any older than you.'

'Oh.' I twisted round to look at her. 'What was it like?'

'Very hard,' said Nana grimly. 'I'd never been away from home before. And I didn't know anyone in Cardiff. I was a nursemaid, and I had to look after two small children, all by myself. They had a mother, of course, but she didn't do much, except give them a kiss when they were bathed and brushed and ready for bed. The father did even less.'

'Did you never get time to play?'

'I had one afternoon and evening off a week.' Nana narrowed her eyes, remembering. 'I used to go to the music hall. I would go on the bus, but I'd walk back along the streets. The lights would be on in the houses, but the curtains were still open, and I'd look in at all the beautiful rooms, with gleaming chandeliers and velvet-covered furniture. *Far* grander than the house where I was working. And I used to hum some of the songs I'd heard while I was out. *Daisy, Daisy, give me your answer do – I'm half crazy, all for the love of you.* The next morning it would be back to scrubbing and cleaning and trying to keep those children in order.'

'Oh Nana…' I swallowed, as I remembered how I'd resented looking after Shirley for even an afternoon.

Nana smiled. 'It's different for you, Megan. You'll have your mum and dad, and your sisters, and you're going to school. You did so well in your exams. We're very proud of you, you know.'

Because that was the astonishing thing. Despite Shirley's accident, and all the upheaval, and feeling really tired the next morning, I had passed my Eleven Plus. I was going to be a grammar school girl.

Then Nana twisted my hair into rags so that it would be curly in the morning. (I protested that there was no need – it wasn't a party, or even Sunday school, just going to see Mum and Dad, but Nana insisted.) And the next morning, beribboned and curled and dressed in our Sunday best, Nana and Grandpa saw us onto the Cardiff train, travelling in care of the guard. I still didn't like to remember their faces, as the train pulled out. And I hadn't been able to bring myself to write anything to Nana – except for a very quick postcard – since.

And now here I was, peering out of the windows at what might be the very same houses that Nana had once walked past, and I hated Cardiff, and I hated school, and I just wished I could be back with her again.

* * *

'Walk, not run, new girl!'

I slowed to a halt. Then I made myself walk with painful slowness through the school gate. Around me were crowds of girls. Even though I'd been here almost a week, nobody stopped and said hello to me. They were all too busy chattering to each other. They weren't unfriendly, exactly, but I didn't feel I fitted in anywhere. I hadn't been to one of the Cardiff primary schools, or learnt the piano, or French, or had tennis lessons; and none of them seemed ever to roller-skate, or play near railway tracks, or do any of the things I liked to do.

Much worse were the teachers. They were strict and sarcastic. Even out of lessons you couldn't relax. There seemed to be rules about everything. They even measured the skirts of our tunics with a ruler – they had to come exactly three inches above the knee when we knelt down. Mine was a trifle too long and they said I'd have to take it up.

I filed in with the rest to assembly. I wasn't expecting anything other than the usual hymns, but directly after the school prayer, the Headmistress, Miss Ainsley-Howells, called one girl to come and stand at the front. While the whole school stared at her, Miss Ainsley-Howells said, 'I am horrified to learn, Valerie, that you were seen on the street this morning, in your school uniform – ' and here she paused, while everyone held their breath – '*talking to a boy!*' There was a delighted gasp. 'Talking to boys while in uniform, in a public place, is not permitted. I have no choice but to award you a conduct mark!'

It was at that point that I heard the girl in front of me mutter to her friend, 'It was only her *brother*, for Heaven's sake!'

I could hardly believe it, although I already knew you weren't allowed to eat in the street in uniform. Or run. I thought sadly back to Llanelli, where there was nothing to stop me running at full tilt with Davy or Tom, chatting happily, while munching an apple or (if we were very lucky) sharing a bag of sweets.

I soon forgot this, though, for the next lesson was P.E. This was worse than anything. I could keep up in lessons, but I've never been good at sports, and when I started wheezing, and tried to explain about my asthma, the awful bully of a P.E. teacher just shouted at the top of her voice, 'Don't make excuses, girl! I've no time for malingerers here. Whatever it was like at your *old* school – ' she sneered at me, as if she could tell at once I wasn't from a posh Cardiff school – 'you won't get away with that here!'

I turned away, still gasping for breath, and working out in my head how many hours it was until going-home time.

* * *

I climbed onto my bus that afternoon, and went to sit near the back. I was feeling very sorry for myself, and I hardly noticed at first when a girl got on and walked towards me. She was wearing the Grammar School uniform and I dimly recognized her as being in my year. Quickly, I glanced away. I'd had enough of school for the moment, and besides, I didn't want her to see the tears in my eyes and think that I was a complete baby.

She seemed to hesitate for a moment as she drew level with me. But when I determinedly stared out of the window, she chose a seat on the other side of the aisle.

My shoulders slumped suddenly. Why had I done that? She'd probably thought I'd deliberately snubbed her. Why did I get everything wrong? I looked sideways to give her a smile, but she was gazing out of the window. Blushing, I looked away, then with fumbling fingers I reached down to get my library book out of my satchel. While I pretended to read, I kept glancing at the girl. There was something about her dark hair and long, oval face. She reminded me of somebody.

When it was time to get off the bus she was still staring hard out of the window.

Chapter Twelve

A New Start

I opened the door of the flat. 'I'm home!' I called.

From the direction of the bedrooms, Mum replied, 'I'm just seeing to the Littlies!'

So some things didn't change. Other things were very different; though. Damp washing hung from every surface, and there was a smell of soaking nappies. The milk and margarine and various crumb-covered plates were scattered on tables and counters. Toys were strewn everywhere. The fire had gone out.

I flung my things on the sofa and picked my way across the room. I'd have to get my snack myself – any ideas of Mum welcoming me with milk and bread-and-butter the way Nana did were already forgotten. I sighed and started putting dirty plates in the sink.

From the bedroom, Mum called, 'Megan, we've no bread – d'you think you could run to the shop?'

And how was your day at school? She couldn't even be bothered to ask. So I ignored her, dumped the things I was holding, and went into my bedroom.

Shirley was lying on the rug, drawing.

'I went to my new school today,' she announced, looking up.

'Me too,' I muttered. 'It was a right wash-out.'

While Shirley chattered on, I started laying things out on the bed. Clean clothes. Underwear. The blue jumper Nana had knitted for me. My teddy. *Swallows and Amazons*. Pam's lucky rabbit foot (not that it had brought me much luck so far).

'What are you doing?' asked Shirley.

'Never mind,' I muttered, adding the half crown coin that Grandpa had given me when I left. Surely that would be enough for the train fare? Then I pulled down my battered suitcase from the top of the wardrobe and started to shove everything inside.

I don't know how long I'd been thinking about it. But suddenly I knew I couldn't stand being in Cardiff a day longer. I was going home. And although I hadn't been consciously planning it, I knew exactly what to pack too.

'I've got a story book,' Shirley announced. She thrust it into my hands. 'Read it!'

I hesitated. I didn't have much time. Then I sat down and read her the story.

She wasn't that bad, really, Shirley. I'd felt different about her, since she'd almost been crushed under Tom's wheels.

Reading to her reminded me of the book I'd brought back from school. It would be something to read on the train.

I went into the living room to find it, and there was Mum, sitting on the sofa with my book open on her lap. *Five Children and It* by E. Nesbit, borrowed from the school library. Mum looked up at me guiltily. 'Oh Megan,' she said, 'I do hope you don't mind. Do you know, I read this when I was your age? And I absolutely loved it!'

'Oh.' I was very taken aback.

'I knocked over your bag, and this fell out, and I picked it up and just read the first page – and somehow it sucked me in. Goodness, but it's been lovely. A whole twenty minutes to myself, reading a book!'

There was something different about Mum at that moment. She looked – well, happier than usual. And younger too, and less harassed. Maybe it was because she didn't have Barbara glued to one hand and Shirley to the other.

'Why don't you keep on reading?'

'I can't. There's so much to do. Barbara's sleeping, but she'll wake up soon.' Mum looked tired again, and older. 'But look at you, in your smart uniform,' she said suddenly. 'Come and tell me about your day.'

'No, you sit there, and I'll get you a cup of tea.' I might almost have giggled, I sounded so like Nana – but I was too sad. I knew now I couldn't run back to Llanelli. It wouldn't be fair. I'd just have to stay here, and make the best of things…including school.

By the time Dad got back, Mum and I had got the flat a bit straighter. Most of the dry nappies had been folded and put away, and the washing-up was done and the counters wiped. I'd even persuaded Shirley to pick up her toys. Still, I knew I'd have to start on my homework soon, and I had no idea what we were going to have for supper.

Dad came in carrying a loaf of bread under one arm and a newspaper-wrapped parcel under the other. The smell gave it away.

'Fish and chips!'

'That's right – to celebrate the end of your first week! Doesn't she look grown-up in her uniform, Gwen?' Dad grinned at me. 'Well, Megan, how was it? You haven't told us much so far. Did you enjoy it? Could you keep up? I'm sure you knocked the socks off them!'

He looked at me eagerly. He'd been working hard at his new job, and we'd hardly had a chance before to talk.

I smiled as brightly as I could and said, 'It was just fine.'

* * *

A few days later, when I got onto the bus to school, I saw the same dark-haired girl sitting next to the window, with her eyes glued to a book. Actually she'd been there before, but I'd always walked past. This time, I stopped next to her.

I took a deep breath. 'Can I sit next to you?'

She looked up, nodded silently, then returned to her book. I sat down and looked sideways at her. Dark hair, long face, dark eyes.

'I think we're in the same year.'

She nodded. I struggled for more to say. 'Are you Jewish?'

She turned and stared at me, astonished. From the expression on her face, I realized how nosy it sounded. And I remembered that Pam had once told me that some people didn't like Jews. Maybe this girl thought I felt the same.

'I'm sorry,' I gabbled. 'I suppose it's none of my business. It's just – the thing is, you remind me of someone, a friend of mine, and I couldn't think why. I just wondered if it was because you were both Jewish.'

'What's she called?'

'It's a he, and you won't know him. He doesn't live in Cardiff. His name's Davy Levenson.'

A slow smile spread across her face. 'He's my cousin.'

She told me that Davy and his mother might be moving to Cardiff. I was really pleased. Suddenly the conversation became much easier. We exchanged names – she was called Judith – and chatted about our homes. It turned out we lived quite close. After a while, I asked, 'What d'you think of school?'

She pulled a face.

'I know,' I said. 'The teachers are really scary. And I don't fit in at all.'

Judith said solemnly, 'The first day, I wanted to run away. But I think some of the teachers are good, if you're interested in the subject. And one of the older girls was very kind to me, yesterday. She said it takes a while to find your feet but most people make friends in the end.'

'Well, I'll look out for you anyway, at break and on the bus.'

Judith nodded. 'Maybe we can help each other with homework. I'm good at languages. I've noticed that you're good at maths.'

I flushed with pleasure. 'I hope so. I'll need to be – and all the sciences too. I want to be a doctor.'

I'd thought she might laugh at me. But Judith nodded, as if she found nothing strange in this at all. One of her aunts had practised medicine, she said, in Germany. And the long bus ride passed more quickly than it ever had before.

We strolled up to school together, my hat dangling casually from one hand. I no longer noticed how imposing the building looked. Nor was I watching the other girls talking – I was too busy talking myself.

'New girl – hats are to be worn, not carried!' snapped a voice. It was Miss Ainsley-Howells. 'Don't let me have to tell you again!'

Instead of jumping, and scuttling away like a scared mouse, I just looked at Judith, shrugged theatrically, and slammed the hat onto my head. Really, I thought, as we strolled on up the drive. Almost, it felt that I belonged.

* * *

That evening I sat down and wrote my first letter home to Nana.

Dear Nana,

It still feels very strange living in Cardiff. I often think about how you must have felt when you came here all those years ago. School is very strict but today I came second from top in maths. Best of all, I've made a new friend...

The Night Run
Bali Rai

Amritsar, India, 1919. A city on the verge of meltdown,
as tensions between the local people
and the British colonial rulers explode.

Arjan Singh learns that his father has been falsely charged
with serious crimes and faces hanging. He sets out on a
perilous mission to save his father, in the face of armed troops,
martial curfew, and vicious local bandits.
Can Arjan escape and get to his father before it's too late?

ISBN 978-1-4729-0436-2   £5.99